P9-BJD-344

Once There Was A Bull... (frog)

By Rick Walton

Illustrated by
Greg Hally

PAPERSTAR

The Putnam & Grosset Group

Printed on recycled paper

Text copyright © 1995 by Rick Walton
Illustrations © 1995 by Greg Hally
All rights reserved. This book, or parts thereof, may not be reproduced
in any form without permission in writing from the publisher.
A PaperStar Book, published in 1998 by The Putnam & Grosset Group,
200 Madison Avenue, New York, NY 10016.
PaperStar is a registered trademark of The Putnam Berkley Group, Inc.
The PaperStar logo is a trademark of The Putnam Berkley Group, Inc.
Originally published in 1995 by Gibbs Smith, Publisher.
Published simultaneously in Canada
Printed in the United States of America
Book design by Traci O'Very Covey
Library of Congress Cataloging-in-Publication Data
Walton, Rick. Once there was a bull—frog / written by Rick Walton;
illustrated by Greg Hally. p. cm.
Summary: A bullfrog in the Old West loses his hop in this lively tale
where each page must be turned to complete the previous image.
[1. Frogs—Fiction.] I. Hally, Greg, ill. II. Title.
PZ7.W17740n 1995 94-32513 [E]—dc20 CIP AC
ISBN 0-698-11607-0
1 3 5 7 9 10 8 6 4 2

Dedicated

to Carolee and Terry Ferris
and all their little hoppers
R.W.

to Daddy's girls, Lauren and Madison
C.H.

Once there was a **bull**...

frog who had lost his hop.

He looked under a **toad**...

stool. But his hop wasn't there.

He looked behind a **dog**…

house. But his hop wasn't there.

He looked under a **hedge**...

hog. But his hop wasn't there.

"Maybe if I jump off something I'll find my hop,"
he said, so he climbed on top of a **box**...

car and jumped!

He landed hard in a patch of *grass*...

hoppers. They hopped away, but Bullfrog didn't.

"Not high enough," said Bullfrog. "Maybe if someone threw me, I'd go high enough to get my hop back." "I'll do it," said a **cow**...

boy, who loved to throw things, and he picked up
Bullfrog and tossed him high and far.

Bullfrog tumbled through the air
and landed in a field of **straw**...

berries. "Oof!" Then he tried to hop.
He couldn't. "Oh, woe," said Bullfrog. "I've lost my hop!"

"Then swim," said a *cat*...

fish from the stream nearby.
"I can't swim on land," said Bullfrog.

"Then fly," said a **lady**...

bug who heard Bullfrog complain. "I can't," said Bullfrog.
"I have no wings. And without wings, flying hurts."

"You could *slither*," said a voice behind Bullfrog.
He turned and looked.
On the ground behind him was a **diamond**...

back rattlesnake looking for breakfast.
"A snake!" croaked Bullfrog.

And up into the air he leaped, higher than the **sun**...

flowers around him. And when he came down,
he leaped again. And again. And again.